NOBODY'S MOTHER is in SECOND GRADE

Robin Pulver · pictures by G. Brian Karas

Dial Books for Young Readers New York

Published by Dial Books for Young Readers
A Division of Penguin Books USA Inc.
375 Hudson Street
New York, New York 10014

Designed by Amelia Lau Carling
Printed in Hong Kong by South China Printing Company (1988) Limited
First Edition
1 3 5 7 9 10 8 6 4 2

Library of Congress Cataloging in Publication Data
Pulver, Robin.
Nobody's mother is in second grade / Robin Pulver;
pictures by G. Brian Karas. —1st ed.
p. cm.
Summary: Cassandra's mother, who wishes she could go to
second grade again, visits her daughter's class disguised as a plant.
ISBN 0-8037-1210-3.—ISBN 0-8037-1211-1 (lib. bdg.)
[1. Plants—Fiction. 2. Mothers and daughters—Fiction.
3. Schools—Fiction.] I. Karas, G. Brian, ill. II. Title.
PZ7.P97325No 1992 [E]—dc20 91-16395 CIP AC

The artwork for this book was prepared with pencil and watercolors.
It was then color-separated and reproduced in full color.

For my ever-loving, plant-loving husband,
my gardening mother and father, and for Nina,
who once again sowed a good story seed
R. P.

To Maximillian and Alexander
B. K.

"$\mathcal{D}$id you go to second grade when you were my age?" Cassandra asked her mother one night at dinner.

"Oh, yes," replied her mother. "I loved second grade so much, I even saved my favorite lunch box. Tell me again, Cassandra, what you like best at school."

"I like stories and singing. I like playground and playacting. I like math too. And our class has a rabbit named Lopsy."

"Lucky Lopsy!" said Cassandra's mother. "I wish *I* could go to second grade again."

Cassandra shook her head. "Nobody's mother is in second grade. That would be ridiculous." Cassandra thought and thought. Then she said, "I know! Miss Gardner loves green plants. She's teaching us about them. You could come to school as a plant!"

"What a good idea," agreed Cassandra's mother. "Tomorrow is my day off. Tomorrow I shall be a second-grade plant!"

Cassandra's mother stayed up late, snipping, fitting, and stitching.

In the morning a beautiful plant gave Cassandra breakfast and fixed two lunches for school.

"Don't tell anyone that you're my mother," said Cassandra. "Nobody's mother is in second grade. That would be ridiculous."

"I won't say a word," promised the plant.

Cassandra and the plant hurried to catch the bus.
The plant's leaves shone in the morning sun.

At school Cassandra told her teacher, Miss Gardner, that she had brought a plant from home.

"How nice!" said Miss Gardner. "The plant can stand next to the window, Cassandra."

Miss Gardner announced, "Class, this is our lucky day. Cassandra has brought us a new plant. Let's welcome it with a song!"

The class sang "You Are My Sunshine" for the plant. It clapped its leaves to the music.

"There's something peculiar about that plant," whispered Kate to Claire when the song was almost done. "I thought I heard it hum!"

Cassandra said, "Miss Gardner, could we let Lopsy out today? The plant was hoping to watch him hop."

"I never knew that watching rabbits hop is something plants like," said Miss Gardner. "I wonder how you know that, Cassandra?"

"I just know," replied Cassandra.

Cassandra let Lopsy out of his cage. Lopsy hopped over
to the plant.

All the way across the room Claire whispered to Kyle,
"There's something peculiar about that plant. I'm sure I
saw it smile!"

Miss Gardner said, "This is the perfect time for our lesson about green plants. How do they help people?"

"Some plants give us shade and shelter," said Kate.

Cassandra thought about her mother putting up the big umbrella at the beach. She thought about her mother fixing a leak in the roof. "This plant gives good shade and shelter," said Cassandra.

PARTS of PLANTS

Leaves

Flowers

Fruit

Stem

Roots

Claire raised her hand. "Plants help the air we breathe."
Cassandra thought about stew steaming on the stove.
"This plant makes the air *smell* good," she said.
"Medicine comes from some plants," said Kyle.
Cassandra remembered her mother giving her medicine
on a spoon. "Medicine comes from this plant too," she said.

"Some plants give us food," said Kim.

Cassandra thought of pancakes and birthday cakes and tacos and spaghetti. "Great food comes from this plant!" she said.

"Plants are pretty to look at," said Chris.

"You should see this plant all dressed up and ready to go out!" exclaimed Cassandra.

"Some plants have flowers," said Clementine.

"This plant grows lots and lots of flowers in the spring," Cassandra said.

"Cassandra," said Miss Gardner, "I wonder how you know so much about the plant you brought to school?"

"I just do," replied Cassandra.

"There's something peculiar about Cassandra's plant,"
said Kevin. "Miss Gardner, it has been looking out the
window all during our lesson."

"Most green plants turn toward light," said Miss Gardner.
"They can't help it."

Cassandra said, "The plant is looking out the window
because it wants to go outside."

"Plants do like fresh air," agreed Miss Gardner. "Let's line
up for playground."

The plant whirled on the merry-go-round. The plant swung
on the swings and bounced up and down on the seesaw.
It climbed on the ladder and hung from the monkey bars.
"I didn't know plants could climb and hang!" said Kate.
"I know lots of hanging plants," said Miss Gardner. "And
many plants climb. Morning glories climb. Poison ivy climbs.
Pole beans are great climbers!"

"But there's something peculiar about that plant," whispered Kyle to Kim, who was way up high on the ladder with him. "It has legs as well as leaves!"

"Maybe Cassandra's plant is a human bean!" said Kim. She laughed so hard, she almost fell off the ladder.

The plant got dirty on the playground.
"Uh-oh," said Kevin. "The teacher's going to be mad."
"I'm not mad," said Miss Gardner. "Dirt is good for plants.
Plants *need* dirt to grow! Come, class, it's time for lunch."

Everyone lined up at the cafeteria. The plant was so excited, it dropped its lunch box. Its lunch fell out. The children helped gather up the sandwich, carrots, and cookie.

Way at the end of the long lunch line, Chris called out to Clementine, "There's something peculiar about that plant. Plants don't eat in the cafeteria!"

"Green plants usually get their food from the soil," Miss Gardner reminded the children. "Our visiting plant is very polite to eat with us in the cafeteria."

After lunch Kevin said, "Miss Gardner, the plant has lost some of its leaves."

"Plants do lose leaves, but they can grow new ones," said Miss Gardner. "This would be a good problem for our math lesson. Listen carefully, class! A plant has twenty leaves. It loses six and grows ten more. How many leaves does it have then?"

"Twenty-four!" shouted the class.

"There's something peculiar about that plant," muttered
Clementine to Claire. "I think it's wearing pants!"
"With flowers," whispered Claire, and she collapsed in
laughter on her chair.

"It is time to act out a story," said Miss Gardner when math was through. "Today's story is 'Jack and the Beanstalk.'"

The plant bounced up and down and waved its leaves.

"Perhaps Cassandra's plant could be our Beanstalk," Miss Gardner said.

Cassandra said, "Miss Gardner, could I please be Jack?"

"Yes," said Miss Gardner. "But don't really climb the Beanstalk. Just pretend. I'm not sure the plant can hold you."

"This plant can hold me very well," replied Cassandra.

"I wonder how you know that?" asked Miss Gardner.

Cassandra thought about the time she fell off her bike and
scraped both knees and her mother carried her home.
She remembered when she had chicken pox on her birthday,
and her mother carried her downstairs for presents and cake.

"I just know," said Cassandra, and she threw her arms around the plant. The plant lifted Cassandra up and hugged her.

"There's something *very* peculiar about that plant!" the children chanted all together.

After "Jack and the Beanstalk" it was time to go home.

"Thank you for bringing your plant, Cassandra," said Miss Gardner. "It's perfect for our second grade. I wish it could stay all year."

"Oh, no!" said Cassandra. "This plant has to go home with me. You see, she's—"

The children chimed in, "She's Cassandra's mother!"

"This plant is Cassandra's mother?" asked Miss Gardner. "I wonder how all of you knew that?"

"We just knew," answered the children.

Miss Gardner turned to Cassandra. "I hope your mother will join our class again. She doesn't have to pretend to be a plant."

"Thank you, Miss Gardner," replied Cassandra. "But nobody's mother is in second grade. That would be ridiculous!"

Pulver, Robin   SCHOOL   JJ
Nobody's mother is in second
grade